TALES FROM TEMPLETON III

TEMPLETON FAMILY ANTHOLOGY

Published by Pen & Publish
Bloomington, Indiana
(812) 837-9226
info@PenandPublish.com
www.PenandPublish.com

ISBN: 978-0-9790446-6-3   ISBN: 0-9790446-6-9
This book is printed on acid free paper.

Printed in the USA

Acknowledgements

We are grateful to the "To the Bell and Beyond" program for making possible the publication of the Templeton Family Anthology. The students, teachers, staff and families of Templeton Elementary School hope you will enjoy their stories, poems and artwork. In addition to providing scholarship support, "To the Bell and Beyond" has provided copies of the Anthology to City of Bloomington officials, the public library, and the Monroe County Community School Corporation elementary school libraries.

Templeton students, staff, and families
Bloomington, Indiana
May 2007

Cover artists: Myles Babcock, Riley Bowles, Simon Brooks, Lucia Davila, Adam Diersing, Toudora Galuska, Walter Guardino, Cordelia Harlow, Vivian Livesay, Jonas Longacre, Becca Smith, Marie Thomas, Randy Vaughn, Stella Winterman, Ben Woolford.

Dive
by Sarah Berry

Dive,
Into the pale blue water
Where the coral grows
And the fish linger.

Where the Sun's rays
Barely touch,
Like the moon's
Soft glow.

It touches only you,
And follows
Wherever you go.

In the pale blue
Water near the
Coral.

Birthdays
by Kacee Vonderschmidt

My birthday is coming soon. It is in fourteen days and two weeks to be exact. I'm turning eight years old. My birthday is on the 27th of September. At my party there is going to be a piñata. It will look like Dora the Explorer.

There will be about twenty of my friends at my party and there will be a cool cake, too. I love birthdays because there are lots of friends. It's not just about the presents. It's all about how much fun you have!

1

Friends
by Kiaundra Dishman

I have two friends;
Our friendship will never end.
Kati and Toni are there
For me any time I need help
Or am in need.
Kati likes pink;
Toni does too.
Toni likes chicken;
Kati likes stew.
Kati is 8;
Toni is 9.
One day I hope you'll find
Great friends like mine!

Nighty-Night Time
(A lullaby dedicated to my baby brother, Garren)
by Kiaundra Dishman

You've been awake all day,
And now I have to say
It's nighty-night time.
Oh, nighty-night time.
Listen carefully: Oh, don't
You believe it's nighty-night time?
If you don't go to bed and don't do
What I said then you'll be the one
In a dream
With a pickle on your head.

Nighty-night time,
Nighty-night time,
Nighty-night time.

Templeton Kittens
by Nancy Soto

One morning last spring as I was walking in to school I saw a group of people gathered around on the sidewalk by the playground. I noticed that they were all looking into the manhole which had the cover off. And down in the hole, up to her neck, was Mrs. Lynas, our school nurse!

When I asked what was going on one of the kids said, "There are two kittens down there and they can't get out! They're crying!" And sure enough, when I listened closely I could hear little tiny mewing cries. Mrs. Lynas climbed back out of the hole saying that the kittens were scared to come out and had gone farther down the pipes. Then somebody's mom offered some pieces of cheese from her child's lunchbox from yesterday.

I volunteered to go down the manhole this time- I really wanted to see those kittens! So I climbed in and crouched down. Fortunately for the kittens and for me too it was dry in there. I looked down the drainage pipe to the left and saw a little gray striped kitten. Down the pipe to the right was a black and white one. They were tiny and scared. But they were also curious about the little pieces of cheese in my hand.

Little by little I coaxed them closer until I could grab them, one at a time, and lift them up out of the hole to the eager hands above. Someone's dad put the manhole cover back on- and the group of rescuers brought the two mewing kittens into the school office.

Everyone was excited to have those two Templeton kittens in the building. Before the school day was over both kittens had been adopted. Ms. Barb, one of our Kindergarten teachers, took the gray one. Her students helped her name him "E.E.". And Olivia and Emily's mother said they could take the black and white one home. They named him "Max".

Now E.E. comes back to visit Ms. Barb's class occasionally. He's grown into a big sweet lap cat who loves attention. Max enjoys a contented life at Emily and Olivia's house, in the company of their other cat. What a lucky day that was for those two lost kittens and the two Templeton families who adopted them!

Nature
by Daniel Davila

Nature is another world where everything lives, but looks different. It's very green and beautiful, and we as humans have no right to kill nature; that means: cutting down trees, stepping on or yanking flowers out of the ground. It's destroying and killing living things. How would you like giant trees attacking you and your families?

We need to take care of nature very good and here are a few reasons why: One, trees give us oxygen; two, plants make earth look beautiful. Now, I do think we need wood from trees to make our houses but I think people should plant when they cut down trees. My point is, don't cut down trees or if you do, plant another one.

Summer's Here
by Hallie Pederson

When the last school bell sounds,
It means summer's around,
And these are sights and sounds you'll hear.
The boys cheer,
And the girls talk in groups so nobody hears,
And the smarty pants ('bout their grades) jeer,
And the bullies bring fear,
And the teachers don't pull ears,
And the warm weather they hold dear,
And the teacher's pets get teary,
Because the end is near,
And they all have an emotion,
Because of this one notion:
They won't see school 'til next year!

What I Will Teach My Baby Brother
by Lucia Davila

I want to teach my baby brother how to do a lot of things when he is born. He will be born in June or May. Anyway, I want to teach him how to read, get dressed, and walk, draw, and jump, and how to play "Slug" (a game that me and my big brother Daniel invented).

I don't think that teaching him how to jump will be too hard or how to draw. He will probably start out drawing with scribbles as all babies do but eventually he should get better at it. And jumping should seem really easy because you could simply hold both of the baby's hands and lift him off the ground until the baby can jump by himself.

It may be sort of hard to teach the baby how to read and get dressed. That's all I have to tell you.

The End.

The Big Book of Daddy Duck
by Stella Winterman and Adam Diersing
Edited by Sierra T. Reed

*Jack be nimble, Jack be quick
Jack jump over the candlestick
Burned his butt on the candle flame
Has to go to the hospital again.

* Hickory dickory punk
The cat fell down with a thunk
The clock went ker-splat
And killed the poor cat,
Hickory dickory punk.

*Hey diddle little
The mouse and the fiddle,
The chicken flew over the sun,
The little pig cried to see such trouble,
And the fork ran away with the knife, and now it's done.

*Blah, blah, red rooster,
Have you any eggs?
No, no, no, no roosters don't lay eggs.

*This little cow went to the butcher,
This little cow ate roast beef,
This little cow got milked by the farmer,
And the first little cow didn't go home.

*Roses aren't red,
Violets are green,
My face is funny,
But yours likes to scream!!!!!

*Bob and Bill
Met Jack and Jill

Climbing up the mountain,
Bob fell down and broke his neck,
And they never saw him after.

*Fummy dummy, stood on the back of the
Empire State building,
Fummy dummy took a lungy jumpy,
Fummy dummy went boomy.

*Once there were three girls and a dad.
The first girl went up and said,
"Daddy, why is my name Rose?"
"Because a rose fell on your head when you were born."
Then the second girl went up and said,
"Daddy, why is my name Daisy?"
"Because a daisy fell on your head when you were born."
Then the last girl staggered up and said in a faint voice,
"Why am I named Cinderblock?"

Night Sky
by Nathan Plew

The stars are bright.
The moon is too
With the wishing star
Being wished on
And being the brightest of all
While the night is dark
Until the day.
And that's all I have to say.

The Little Kid Who Believed He Could Be a Football Player
by Anthony Keene

Once upon a time, there was a little kid who believed he could play for the Indianapolis Colts. His dad played football for the Indianapolis Colts and he wanted to keep playing. But his dad would never pay attention to his son and the son was getting really sad because his dad would never have time for him. So he left and he never came back.

Fifteen years later, he was playing football for his school and he won all his games and he was so good he got drafted into the NFL by the Indianapolis Colts. He was so happy, he moved to Indy to play on the team.

So one day he had to meet the coach, Tony Dungy. After he met the coach, he had to meet his teammates, including Marvin Harrison, Peyton Manning, and Dominic Rhodes. His coach made him another running back to team up with Dominic Rhodes.

Then their first game came, against the Cincinnati Bengals, and after the first quarter, the score was tied up at 23-23. So he ran to Adam Vinatieri because he had to kick a 43-yard field goal. And he told him to kick it to the left because the wind was blowing at least 10 mph. And then the fourth quarter ended and the score was 43-25, and the Colts won.

And the kid played six more successful seasons, winning two super bowls and becoming the league MVP once. Five years later, he was inducted into the hall of fame. He lived happily ever after.

A Prank for Mommy
by Cyan Michal Carey (and mom, Esther)

On one cool February day Cyan and her baby brother Israel Robin were playing in their room. Israel was getting ready to walk at any time. He was almost one year old.

Mommy was in the kitchen fixing dinner when all of a sudden Cyan yells out, "Mommy, Mommy! Israel walked!" Mommy ran into the room as fast as she could and there was Israel standing on the other side of the room, opposite of where he was just a few minutes ago.

"Oh my goodness!" Mommy screamed with delight! I cannot believe it. Israel walked! Then all of a sudden she looked at sweet Cyan with a grin on her face and Cyan said, "I'm just joking. I put him on the other side of the room."

"What a good prank, Cyan. You're taking after Mommy, and you got me good."

Then Mommy and Cyan laughed and hugged and Israel crawled over to be part of the hug as well. It was a very funny prank that mommy would never forget.

The End

Oh Beautiful Things
by Kevin Vosburgh and Basie Cobine

Oh, oh, oh beautiful, so sleek, so fast, and dogs scare you. You go so fast but don't complete every task. So bold yet so meek. You have dug deep into my heart. So utterly maddening yet you still make me smile. Oh great little furry (one) you always like to scurry. You like to eat tuna, chicken, and catfish too. Cats are keen. Cats are great. Cats are clean. They lick your plate. You are very, very furry. White, black, brown, and orange too. The mice are your playthings. Your eyes are so bright. Also they shine. You can climb so high you seem to touch the sky. You enjoy watching birds and rabbit chasing. What am I? I am a cat.

9

The Big Thunder
by Shahzadi Upadhyay

One day I woke up
I looked
I saw rain
I couldn't go outside
On my favorite day
Which was Friday
I had a cat
She could tell me
The weather
Because I was
Sick.

My mother got me soup
And milk
My tooth hurt
In my bedroom
My first taste
My tooth fell
Into the soup.

My cat peeks out
Of her little door, says
"Someone is hurt
In the little rain."
I say: Save him from the big thunder.
Give me the phone, Cat. No one can hear
In the world, and so I have to scream
To tell everyone.

Hello! Whoever owns that man
Take him home
Put him on the couch
Throw him a blanket
A pillow
Feed him some soup.

by Lance Green-Hogue

This super car of the police catches the super car. The super car will beat this...... day.

by Keilan McVicker

One winter day, the angel was flying. The robber stole the girl's money. The angel took the money back. The angel gave the money to the girl.

by MaKinsey Pitman

Two dancing princesses are dancing. She threw up.

by Nathan Baumgardner

I am a mechanic. The tires came off. The customer says "That's O.K."

Bob and the Pink Ford Truck
by Adam Diersing

Once upon a time there was a guy named Bob. He owned a pink Ford truck and his family always laughed at him. "I don't care what you say," he always said "I like my pink Ford truck."

"Ha, ha, ha," they said.

"Good-bye," he said.

One day he found

A pink bunny behind his truck "what the heck!!!" he said

"Oh, it's a pink bunny I love stuff that's pink," so he kept the bunny.

And they all lived happily never before.

11

Don't Let the Pigeon Drive the Wacker-Backer
by Eliah ben Zayin and Zayin

Once upon a time, deep in the heart of Africa where the grassland meets the jungle, there was a very special place called the Pridelands. And right in the center of the Pridelands was a very unusual rock formation called Pride Rock. At the top of Pride Rock was a cave and that cave was the home of a very unusual lion cub named Simba. Simba lived in the cave at the top of Pride Rock with his mother Serabi and his poppa Mufasa. He also had a very unusual friend named Eliyah. Eliyah was a little boy that lived in a grass hut he built down by the monkey stage near the water hole. Eliyah was the King of Pepperoni, magicians and inventors. He and Simba had very unusual friends. They were Baby Dragon and Baby Frill Snake. They liked pepperoni too.

One morning Eliyah was eating his pepperoni Lucky Charms [R] when suddenly there was a Knock! Knock! Knock! at the door. Eliyah said, "What-ca-day me-uh in," which is a very silly thing to say but that's what he said.

The door opened and there stood the pigeon. And what do you think the pigeon said?

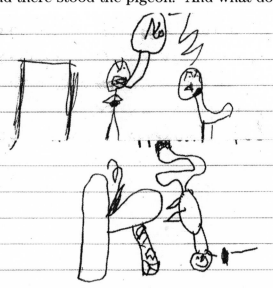

The pigeon said, "Eliyah, can I borrow your Wacker-backer?"

And Eliyah said, "No! You did not say please and besides that you wrecked my bulldozer because you don't even have hands to steer with!"

The pigeon said, "Oh man!" and

stomped out the door.

Eliyah was just finishing his breakfast when there was a Knock! Knock! Knock! at the door. Eliyah said, "Pigeon, don't come in again!" But when the door opened it wasn't the pigeon, it was Simba. And Simba was mad.

Eliyah said, "What happened to you?" And Simba said, "I got wacked in the back by a pigeon attack."

Just at that moment came a Knock! Knock! Knock! at the door. Eliyah said, "Pigeon, you shouldn't wack folks in the back!" But when the door opened it was Baby Frill Snake with a cross-eyed dizzy look. And Eliyah said, "What happened to you?"

Baby Frill Snake said, "I got wacked in the head by a pigeon."

Eliyah asked him where the pigeon was now but Baby Frill Snake said, "I don't know. He wacked me from the back and ran away.

Just then came a Knock! Knock! Knock! at the door. Eliyah said, "Come in!" Who do you suppose was at the door? It was Baby Dragon, holding his knee and saying, "Ow, ow, ow!" Eliyah asked what was wrong and Baby Dragon said, "I got wacked in the knee by a pigeon attack." Eliyah asked him where the pigeon went but Baby Dragon said, "I don't know. He wacked me from the back and ran away."

Well, right about now Eliyah was beginning to get irritated about the pigeon's misbehavior. He went outside to look for the pigeon when WHACK! Something wacked Eliyah's back. The pigeon had smacked Eliyah's back with his wing and laughed at Eliyah. Eliyah turned to face the pigeon and the pigeon said, "Uh-oh...." And then he ran away. That's when Eliyah grabbed the keys to the Wacker-backer, jumped in and fired it up. Not many people have ever heard of a Wacker-backer. Even fewer have ever seen one. And you can bet no one wants to see a Wacker-backer from the business end of its brooms, flyswatters and various bits of rotating junk.

Eliyah drove off looking for the pigeon. After a while he decided to get back out and check for pigeon tracks and it was right then that the pigeon crept up and jumped inside. The pigeon didn't know how to control the Wacker-backer so what do you think he did? He turned all the keys and pulled the lever for the solar panels and what did he hear? It was the sound of the engine starting and rumbling like thunder and humming like a million bees. *Ku-chunk-ch-ch-ch-ch* and *vroom* and then the Wacker-backer started moving, and the brooms started sweeping and the flyswatters started swatting and the popguns started popping. It was a horrible loud noise. Did Eliyah hear it? Yes he did! And Baby Frill Snake heard it. And Baby Dragon heard it and Simba heard it too. That's when they all took off in the Bo-bo ship to catch the Wacker-backer. The pigeon could not control the Wacker-backer. It was knocking down the club house. It was running over trees and monkeys (poor little things). It was a mess.

Eliyah and his friends chased the pigeon to his hide-out. The Wacker-backer was running over the pigeon's hide-out and Eliyah jumped out with a big stick and shoved it into the Wacker-backer's gears to make it stop. Then he pried on the stick so hard it shot the pigeon clear out of the Wacker-backer into the air and into the back of the Bo-bo ship. Baby Dragon and Baby Frill Snake and Simba caught the pigeon. They shrank the pigeon with Shrink Inc. machine and put him in a jar. And they never had trouble again.

The end.

Colts vs. Bears
by Lain Stocke

I went to Lee's house to watch the Super Bowl. There were six of my friends there. I was playing pool and it was really fun. During the game I was playing video games.

I came in the room and I saw the Colts kick the ball and the Bears got it. They ran and got a touchdown.

It was sweet when the Colts won! I had to go home but I got a piece of cookie cake.

The end

Peace
by Heather Harlow

I wish for world peace,
I dream of world peace,
I imagine world peace,
But peace will never come.

Too many wars,
Too many fights,
Too many long nights,
And peace will never come,
Peace will never come.

The grass will grow
The flowers bloom,
But all I hear is one loud boom!
I feel like peace will never come,
Peace will never come.

I wish for world peace,
I dream of world peace,
I imagine world peace,
But peace will never come,
Peace will never come.

The Jaguar
by Rebecca Elliott

Shh, shh, I heard the jaguar
Is coming today.
Shh, shhh, It's right beside me!
Oh! It's just my kitten. Good bye.

Historias de Ficcion y Aventuras
de Richy Seyberts

Fictional Stories and Adventures
by Richy Seyberts

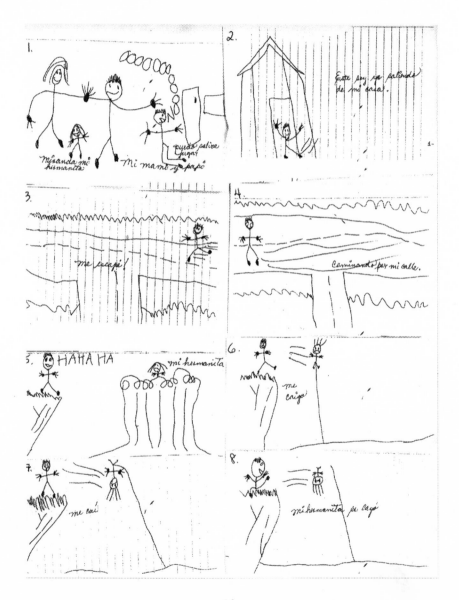

1. Miranda, my little sister. My mommy and daddy. "Can I go out to play?"
2. This is me leaving my house.
3. I escaped!
4. Walking down my street.
5. Ha ha ha! My little sister.
6. I am falling.
7. I fell.
8. My little sister fell.

9. My Grandma.
10. Me thinking so many things in my head.
11. Animals of the earth and the air.
12. The Dragon of the Sea.
13. This is me when I am big and very strong.
14. Me sleeping.

15. Valentine's Day. My mommy and I!
16 and 17. This is my sea. I am looking through my telescope, fight with pirates, dragons, octopuses, eels. I am surfing.
18. When I don't want to do homework!
19. My little sister. We call her "Mini". "Mini" because she is very mischievous.

Poke Poem
by Alex Frey

Growlithe
    learns
        flame thrower
           a
             level
               4a
                &
                 he
                  has
                 a
                  really
                    tough
                      spine.

He
    used
        flame thrower
            on
          a
            piloswine
              &
               hurt
                his
                 little
                  spine.

Poem
by Jeff, Deb, Will and JD McMillian

Big
Umbriferous
Cuddly
K-9

One hundred thirty pounds
Ubiquitary
Rags

Glacial
Riiiiiiiiip!
Eats a lot
Agile
Tug master

Playful
Yucky drool
Run sweeper daily

Poem
by Ben Webb

Gyrados
Learns hyper beam
And Charizard looks very mean.
And even known they're both dragon types.
They both don't look a lot alike.
But they're also opposite types
'Cause water hurts fire type
But I'm finished so,
You can stop reading
And start to go.

Diary
by Kalien Vaughn

Dear Diary,

Hi, I'm Lisa and this is my diary. WARNING: Some things might sound a little weird only if Kelly did it. If your name is Kelly don't pass this point.

August 1st

Dear Diary,

Today was the first day back to school. Kelly was there and mean as usual. She found toilet paper stuck to her shoe and she blamed it on me. Why would she blame it on someone who secretly did do it? I also saw Daisy at my school. Daisy is Kelly's dog. Daisy is a Chihuahua. Most of the time Chihuahuas have big ears and small bodies. Well, Daisy has small ears and a big body. Kelly makes Daisy wear stupid fuzzy outfits. Kelly doesn't know this but Daisy buries her doggy clothes.

August 2nd

Dear Diary,

Today was perfect but my dog Holly got in a fight with Daisy. Holly won because Daisy's fat. And Holly stays in shape.

August 3rd

Dear Diary,

I finally defeated Kelly in a staring contest. So now there's nothing to write about. Except, P.S. Kelly, sorry you had to find out about the doggy clothes.

The end!

Birthday Party
by Julia Boorkland

Happy people, dancing, laughing
Eating lots of birthday cake.
Opening presents, playing, jumping
Having lots of fun with friends.
This birthday party never ends.

My Pony Cokie
by Kelsey Todd

I have a pony named Cokie. I ride her in the summer and spring. I went to the Saddle Club last year with my friends Lauren and Bobbi Jo. Lauren has a pony named Rosie, but Bobbi Jo doesn't have a pony.

Rosie was on one side of the arena. Cokie was on the other side. Rosie started to run to the other side where Cokie was. Then we went outside to the bigger arena. Lauren and I had a race. I won. Then Lauren won. We went home and rode in the back of the barn out back. We had fun.

The end

Squishy Peanut Butter
by Enrique Galindo

I ate peanut butter.

It crawled

    down

    down

      down

   my

  LONG

    Dark

   throat.

      squish

        squash

      squish

        squash

      squish

  KURPLUNK

into my belly.

The acid *shriveled*

my brown

   squishy

   peanut butter.

Going to Kiana's House
by Tasia Todd

On Saturday I went skating. It was fun. I went to Kiana's. We played to 11:00. We went to Nick's room to watch a movie we were going to watch - a scary movie. But Kissy said, "No!" So we just watched another movie.

In the morning we got up and got dressed for church. At 9:30 the church came to pick us up. After church we went back to Kiana's house and played games until 3:00 p.m. Kissy went to church. We were at Kissy's house until 1:00 by ourselves. Me and Kiana played games. At 4:00 p.m. Kissy came back in to do Kiana's hair.

At 5:00 p.m. Kiana got up and we went inside. Outside we made a house. I got cut by a point. I got a Band-aid. Kiana got cut too by a stick. After that at 9:00 p.m. I had to go home.

The end

Fish Bone Stuck in Mom's Throat
by Benny Luo

My mom and I went to the Dragon Express Chinese Restaurant. My mom bought some fish, and then we came home after that. My mom got the fish bone stuck in her throat when she tried to eat the fish and did not grind up the fish bone. Oh, no! She choked on the fish bone and didn't spit it out. Luckily, an ambulance did not have to come, because she was going to get the fish bone out. She coughed and she got the fish bone out. I am very glad that my mom got the fish bone out. I think it's very funny.

The end

Head Lice
by Simon Schönemann-Poppeliers and Daniel Davila

Head lice are scarier than a herd of mice
They're contagious and strong
So please, please don't handle them wrong
For these little beings aren't to be seen by your seeings
They eat at your skin with a nasty grin
And after awhile you won't have a smile
for those rotten pests
Have gotten the best of you for a long long while.

How to Be a Good Husband
by Ready, Set, Grow Pre-school~ Templeton

To be a good husband you should......
>Drive safely.   (Noah)
>Marry someone pretty like a rock star. (Jack)
>Be a boy with a suit, that's all. (Melody)
>Make people happy. (Mora)
>Need a baby and baby stuff. (Salinger)
>Fix things. (Joel)
>Be nice and like the presents she gives you.   (Sam R.)
>Fix the cracks in the ceiling so the bugs don't come in. (Adam)
>Let her lay her head on your lap. (Lily)
>Be a good daddy. (Brooklyn)
>Always be happy. (Roxy)
>Have a job with money. (Alexi)
>Do work in the yard. (Cayden)
>Like the mom. (Hara)
>The wife does nothing; the man does everything. (Mason)
>Love your wife. (Sam C.)

The Reason I like Drawing
by Michael Bruner

The reason I like drawing
is that when I read a book
with no illustrations I can draw
what I'd think it would look like.

The reason I like books
is you have to find the right one
that makes you not want to stop reading.

Reading a book brings you into a whole new adventure –
one where you don't know which is the real world or which is not.

Diddle Dum
by Daniel Davila and Simon Schönemann-Poppeliers

Diddle dum went walking as happy as can be
But as he returned he couldn't find his peas
He looked up down and all around
Then he thought "Maybe they're near my goat!"
And then he remembered
"Oh Silly me they're down my throat!"

Sue
by Lucia Davila

Sue was 20 years old and she lived in a fish bowl. But she
was not a fish. She was a hamster. She loved water. Her favorite
drink was light blue lemonade. She had a pet ostrich. Her ostrich
laid 523 eggs every week. Her favorite food was Swiss cheese
with ketchup. She liked bananas with banana pie.

Stopping
by Olivia Dagley

Feel the earth
On your feet

               Mother nature
                  Is calling you

What's stopping you?

               Feel the fresh
                    Fresh
        Air
Go to the lake

                   Watch it

It's so free
Swimming around

                    In its
           Freedom
Go to the forest

                Take a hike

Watch the nature

              Go into a life
              Of an animal
Love

                Mother
         Nature

Puppies and Kitties
by Sammy Bunton

Puppies and kitties are young
Puppies and kitties are playful
Puppies and kitties can behave
Puppies and kitties are nice
Puppies and kitties are soft
Puppies and Kitties

Baldzol
by Jonas Longacre

Once upon a time there was a horseback rider. He was riding along and he saw a tower with a bald girl inside. "Rapunzel," said the horseback rider.

"Who is that?" asked the girl

"You!!!" the horseback rider said.

"No, I'm her great, great, great, great, great, great, great, great grandson," she (he) said.

"But I thought you were a girl."

"No! How could you think such a thing!!" she said.

"Wait; I forgot to introduce myself," he said, while bowing. "My name is Gilet."

"Well, I am Baldzol, you idiot!!" the girl said.

"So, do you have anything to get me up the tower?" Gilet asked.

"No, you idiot! My last boyfriend pulled all my hair out and it won't grow back!! Although, I do have a ladder," Baldzol said. So Baldzol got the ladder and set it out of the window. "Here. Climb up this," she said.

And right when he was on the last step, the ladder fell, crushed him, and killed him.

Well, that was the end of him.

The end

Dogs and Cats
by Sammy Bunton

Dogs are tall, cats are small
Dogs can jump, cats can climb
Dogs can play with people; cats can play with yarn or mice
Dogs are pretty, cats are lovable
Dogs and Cats

Jam to the Center of the Earth
An original play
by Lizzy Canada, Lori Canada, Eli Diersing, Dena El Saffar, Amy Flanigan, Bailey Hull, Breshaun Joyner, Ellie Komoda, Layli Komoda, Arielle Moir, Ben Moir, Jamil Moore, Layla Moore, Asher Nottingham, Katcha Papesh, Ronna Papesh, Ivy Richardson, Sheania Robertson, Rebecca Smith, Katherine Sylvester, Lauren Sylvester, Abby Towell, Julie Vonderschmidt, Kacee Vonderschmidt, Amy Waggoner, Hanna Waggoner, Charlie Wagner, Max Williams, Brian Winterman, Esther Winterman, Stella Winterman, Una Winterman, and Families

SCENE ONE

Sounds of crowds cheering, clapping, and stamping their feet.

DIVINE
You've been a great audience. We gotta go. Thank you all. We love you!! Good night!

Curtains open. The stage is divided into two areas. The train platform and the train car. The train platform has two signs. One sign reads Track Four – Little Rock, Lima, Laredo, Lahaina . The other sign reads Track Five – Denver, Dakar, Damascus. On the platform is a man with dark glasses and a briefcase (or suitcase). He is facing the Track Five sign. A fat hamster (GERALD) also wears glasses and a felt hat. He is facing the Track Four sign. Another person obviously dressed as an athlete – a swimmer (LIZZIE). She is practicing swimming strokes. Occasionally she takes deep breaths and holds it.

There is a roped off section marked V.I.P. A "geeky" looking person in a train uniform stands in front of it. She has a <u>large</u> name tag that says "Hi! My name is Myron"

In the train car there are several seats. Only one person (GABBY) is sitting. She is slumped in a chair sleeping.

The band The Volcanoes and their manager walk onstage to the platform area.

29

DRACO

Finally! I thought the audience would never stop.

KEITH

They love us. We had to keep playing.

DRACO

It was 75 encores!? I'm glad I booked this show at the Train Stop Auditorium. We can just get on the train and head to the next show.

BOB

Hey dude, where are we going?

DRACO

Don't you ever pay attention when I'm talking? *(Pause)* Where did I say we were going? *(looks into his palm pilot or notebook)* Oh, that's right. Lahaina, Hawaii

BOB

Maui baby!

DRACO

Our train leaves in 10 minutes from track four.

DIVINE

This says track four.

DRACO

Perfect. *(Pulls out his cell phone and begins to talk to **MARGE**)* Hey Marge, all of the equipment better be packed and loaded onto the train in five minutes. *(Pauses)* I don't care if it's going to take you 30 minutes. You only have five! *(Pauses)* Look Marge, we are about to travel on the Charging Chunnel Choo Choo. This is the first all terrain super train. We'll travel over regular train tracks, right through mountains, and under water. We can't afford to miss this train. *(Pause)* You what??? Oh alright, I'll be right there *(closes cell phone)*. I have to solve another crisis.

Here are your tickets. Get on the train and wait for me. You guys are in the V.I.P. section. I'm going to check on the gear *(walks offstage)*.

MYRON, the train attendant takes down the rope to let the band on the train.

KEITH
I want a window seat. Makes me feel alive *(begins to walk onto the train VERY slowly)*

BOB
(teasing)
You're just glad you're <u>still</u> alive.

KEITH
Very funny. You're just jealous because you'll never live to be as old as I am.

DIVINE
Hey your birthday's next week. We'll be in Hawaii for your birthday old man *(gets to his seat and sits down)*.

KEITH
Yep. I'll be 106 years old. Sure wish my mother could be there to see it.

BOB
When did she pass away *(gets to his seat and sits down)*?

KEITH
(offended)
She ain't dead. She's just gonna be in Vegas visiting her parents *(finally reaches his seat)* Aaaaah. A window seat *(takes a long time to sit down)*.

GERALD
Mmmm good! This train stop pizza is great *(Pause, looks at LAUREN)* I said this trainstop pizza is great!

LAUREN

Never touch the stuff. It gives me indigestion. Or maybe it's acid reflux. Maybe both.

GERALD

You're really missing something. Spicy pepperoni and olives is my favorite. *(Pauses, notices LIZZIE)* What about you? *(Pauses, LIZZIE is doing her exercises and not paying attention).* Hey you! You don't like pizza *(puts slice into LIZZIE's face).* Huh?

LIZZIE

I'm on a diet.

GERALD

A diet! You're nothing but skin and bones. Now some say I need to be on a diet *(pats stomach and takes a bite of pizza)* but I like my size. Why don't you eat?

LIZZIE

I'm an athlete – a swimmer. I'm on a diet for my sport.

LAUREN
(walks over to LIZZIE)

Excuse me, did you say swimmer's ear? That's probably what I have *(Pauses)* Although I also think I'm going deaf.

GERALD
(ignoring LAUREN)

What about chocolate? Everybody loves chocolate. I LOVE chocolate pizza.

LIZZIE

I like chocolate but I can't have it because of competition. I'm swimming at the Ivy Springs Invitational in Lima, Peru.

LAUREN

Did you say poison ivy? *(begins to scratch)* That must be why I'm itching.

GERALD

You're fine! I don't see anything. *(turns to **LIZZIE**)* I've had that Laredo pizza. Oh yeah. Tex-mex pizza is the best.

LAUREN

I know it's poison ivy or poison oak or chiggers or something *(begins to scratch violently)*.

CONDUCTOR CARL

(enters from stage left through the train car to the beginning of the train platform)

All Aboard! This train takes the track in t-minus ten minutes.

GERALD

(sings in a blues type voice)

I'm goin' get on the train. Yeah, yeah. Gonna get on the train, and ride it 'til it goes no mo. Yeah, yeah. *(begins to walk on the train, past **KEITH**)*

KEITH

Somebody get rid of that rat!

BOB

*(taps **KEITH**'s shoulder and sits down)*

Chill man. That's not a rat.

GERALD

(begins to sing a blues song)

I'm a hamster
I'm a hamster baby.
A real live chunky hamster
And not some fluffy dancer.

DIVINE

*(walks on the train past **KEITH**)*

Not a bad voice mate. Where are you headed?

GERALD

First stop Memphis for the Beale Street Blues Festival then Chicago for the All Star Blues Showcase *(extends his paw to DIVINE)* Gerald Jones.

DIVINE

Have you heard of The Volcanoes? I'm the lead singer.

GERALD

Oh I'm not into the heavy metal, just blues *(takes out a harmonica and begins to play)*.

DIVINE

Wait until you hear us. We're a whole new sound. Take a seat. *(DIVINE motions for GERALD sit next to him))*.

DRACO
(enters quickly from stage right with MARGE)
If I wasn't in charge, this band would still be playing birthday parties in Bloomington, IN.

MARGE
I told you I could handle it.

DRACO
Right and we'd be in Hawaii and the speakers would be in Zimbabwe.

As *DRACO* and *MARGE* walk quickly to the train, *DRACO* bumps into *LAUREN* and turns him around away from Track Five. *DRACO* does not apologize.

LAUREN

What was that? Oh no. Whiplash. I have whiplash. *(Pauses)* No this feels more like a spinal cord injury *(begins to walk as if in pain off stage right)*.

MARGE

You're in charge of the band. I'm in charge of the gear. Stay out of my way!

DRACO

Don't forget who pays your salary! Wait a minute. Who does pay your salary? Never mind. Just do what I say and...

MARGE

You know if it weren't for me, this band would still be playing birthday parties in Bloomington, Indiana.

DRACO

I got you this job and this is the thanks I get?

MARGE and DRACO sit down still arguing

CONDUCTOR CARL

All aboard. Closing call for the Charging Chunnel Choo Choo. Little Rock, Laredo, Los Angeles, Lahaina and all points in between.

MORGANA
(offstage)

Wait!! Wait!! *(runs onstage)* I can't miss the train! I can't miss the train!! *(hops on stage in a bucket)* Is this the train that The Volcanoes are on?

CONDUCTOR CARL

Better believe it. *(mutters)* Bothersome boogie band boys on board!

MORGANA

Oh I made it just in time *(bumps into **LAUREN** who turns around facing Track Four)*. Oh I'm sorry. I have to get on the train before it leaves. *(Hops on the train and sits in a chair in the back. She tries not to be seen)*

LAUREN

The train's leaving? I'm on my way to the lung specialist in Denver. Wait, wait! Oh no! I feel a cough spasm coming on *(she begins to cough violently which drives him onto the train). MYRON takes down the ropes and V.I.P. sign and places them*

*in the back of the train. While his back is turned CALABAR
and her assistant CALABARBIE slink onstage trying not to be
seen and sneaks onto the back of the train car.   As they sneak
on, CALABAR trips over GABBY who yawns.*

CALABAR
(mumbles)

Excuse me.

GABBY
(picks up cell phone and dials it)

Oh hi Barbie. Sorry I lost you back there for a minute. I fell
asleep. I have all these tests and papers to write for school. And
then there's the pep rallies and parties. Speaking of parties, uh
huh…uh huh…really, *(yawns)* wow…LOL

KEITH

Did ya'll see that girl? She looks familiar.

BOB

Oh you're eyes are getting old.

KEITH

I just bought new glasses and I can see anything - including that
girl. And that girl was Calabar.

DRACO

Who?

KEITH

Calabar is on the train.

DIVINE

I haven't seen her since we kicked her out of the band.

MARGE

She was a lot of trouble. I can take a look around if you want.

DRACO
No I'm sure it is not her…what's her name again? Never mind. I'm sure she's not here. She wouldn't dare try to hurt you guys. At least not for the second time.

CONDUCTOR CARL
(enters and motions for LAUREN to sit down)
Safety saves souls. *(LAUREN sits down. CONDUCTOR CARL walks through the train)*

GABBY
Something doesn't look right *(pulls on CONDUCTOR CARL'S sleeve)* WAM Mr. Conductor, how much longer until we reach Lafayette?

CONDUCTOR CARL
Left Lafayette at 'leven o'clock. 'Tis ten 'til two now.

GABBY
OMG, we're past Lafayette? Oh no! Barbie. CYA *(Dials phone)* Hi Samantha. Listen I fell asleep and missed my stop. I'll call you at the next station and you can pick me up there OK? So tell me about the movie. Was it good? Uh huh…uh huh. What were the special effects like? Uh huh..uh huh *(yawns, falls asleep)*

CONDUCTOR CARL
Tickets! Tickets! Taking tickets! *(CONDUCTOR CARL takes GABBY's ticket.. He turns to LAUREN.)* Ticket!

LAUREN
Here you go. It's in Braille because I'm blind. Could you tell me how long to Denver? I'm seeing a lung specialist there. I also can't sit too long. My tailbone is highly sensitive to sitting in awkward positions. Do you possibly have a pillow I could sit on? No goose down or synthetic material, please. I have allergies.

CONDUCTOR CARL
Sorry maam.

LAUREN

Maybe just a hot water bottle then? But make it lukewarm please. I burn easily.

CONDUCTOR CARL

Terrible ticket. You want Denver Dakar Damascus Depot. This train is Little Rock, Lima, Laredo, Lahaina.

LAUREN
(horrified)

What? I'm on the wrong train!! What am I going to do? Oh no, my heart. I think I'm having a heart attack.

Sound effect of train getting faster and faster, then finally a train whistle. Black out. Curtain close.

SCENE TWO

*Curtains open to reveal the same train but it now takes up the entire stage. On a small section on stage left sits a cart with food, plates, and cups. **COO COO** – The Dining Car Attendant enters from stage left into the train car limping.*

COO COO

Welcome to the Charging Chunnel Choo Choo. My name is, well never mind what my name is. I can't tell you. You don't need to know it anyway. I'm here to take your food orders *(speaks to **GERALD**)* Sir, what would you like?

GERALD

What kind of pizza do you have?

COO COO

Pepperoni, sausage and Hawaiian with ham and pineapple.

GERALD
I'll take all three.

COO COO
(writes on her tablet)
Okie dokie, that's three slices.

GERALD
No silly *(pats stomach)* That's three pizzas!

*(**MORGANA** begins to secretly move down the aisle towards the band. She tries not to be seen).*

COO COO
*(turns to **DIVINE**)*
And your order?

DIVINE
I'll have the Taco N Bag. Extra salsa. It's good for the vocal cords.

COO COO
*(turns to **KEITH**)*
For you?

KEITH
You have anything vegetarian?

COO COO
(sneezes and speaks suspiciously)
Why do you ask? Who told you we had vegetables? Who sent you?

KEITH
Well do you or don't you?
COO COO
This is a meat only food service train here.

KEITH

Only meat! Just bring me a glass of soy milk. Lucky, I brought my own healthy, organic, 100% wheat and gluten free, macrobiotic lunch. How do you think I got to be 105 years old? Surely it wasn't for eatin' Chicken Fries and Mini Corn Dogs all my life! *(takes out a paper bag, pulls out a sandwich and begins to eat)*

DRACO

I'll have the Chicken Fries.

MARGE

I'll have the Mini Corn Dogs, extra mustard. Good lotion for the hands.

COO COO

And you maam *(she surprises MORGANA)?*

MORGANA
(whispers)

No, no, nothing for me at all.

COO COO

Are you sure? We have fish sticks. Oh and the popcorn shrimp is delicious. First, we dip them in batter and drop them into a pot of boiling oil, then...

MORGANA

NO!

(The band looks back at her, realizes who she is and points.)

BOB, DIVINE, KEITH, MARGE, and DRACO

It's her!

CALABAR
(enters stage left and crouches behind the food cart with CALABARBIE)

Now is my chance to get those "musicians" who think they can kick me out of the band and not have to pay for it. You stuck by me Calabarbie as my able assistant all this time. Thank you. *(They hug)* Those awful Volcanoes even have the nerve to record "Jam to the Center of the Earth". That's one of my greatest songs! <u>And</u> it's one of their best selling records. Now it is time for my greatest revenge.

First, I'll put a sleeping potion in everyone's food and drink so no one gets in my way *(begins sprinkling powder on everyone's food and all of the food in the pantry)*. When they wake up they'll find themselves not in a comfortable train station...but the center of the Earth *(evil laugh)*.

The Earth's core is the source of the planet's magnetic field. So that big metal train will be stuck down there forever. They'll never escape *(evil laugh)*.

COO COO
What are you doing back here

CALABAR
(disguises his voice)
Oh nothing. We were looking for the bathroom.

COO COO
It's on the next level.

CALABAR
Thank you *(exits with **CALABARBIE**)*

***CONDUCTOR CARL** and **MYRON** enter*

COO COO
Hello Conductor Carl. What can I get for you tonight? The usual?

CONDUCTOR CARL
Malted milk with melted marshmallows.

COO COO

Your usual Myron?

MYRON

Italian Dunkers.

COO COO

Coming right up.

COO COO gets the cart and fills it with food. She begins to deliver the food down the aisle, sneezing occasionally. Once she finishes, she hands CONDUCTOR CARL his food. CONDUCTOR CARL offers her a marshmallow. She eats it. Everyone begins to get a little woozy.

LIZZIE

I don't feel so good.

COO COO

Who says my food is not good? Is there a secret food critic on board?

LIZZIE

Oh no, the food tastes good but *(yawns)* but I'm drowsy. I've never felt so –

BOB

Sleepy!

DIVINE

I feel kind of drowsy myself.

KEITH
(yawns)
It's not time for my power nap yet.

Everyone collapses. CALABAR enters and looks around at all the bodies sleeping and laughs)

CALABAR

Now I'll steer the train into the giant anthill left of Laramie. Down, down, down into the center of the earth. *(evil laugh)* Then I'll make my way up to the surface of the planet *(does not notice **GABBY**))*.

GABBY
(yawns)
SRY, I fell asleep again Samantha. So as I was saying…

CALABAR

Once I arrive topside, I'll tell the whole world I created the sound of The Volcanoes. Then I'll launch my world concert series. Calabar: The Molten Lava Tour. I'll start off my first show in Cairo at the feet of the Sphinx. Then on to Rome, Nairobi, London, Barstow *(walks off stage still shouting names of cities)* Wichita, Mexico City, Martinsville…

GABBY

Samantha, Samantha…. Darn. I lost the signal *(looks around, sees food next to her)* Ooooh. Taco N Bag. *(takes a bite)* Uh oh. *(immediately falls asleep)*

Blackout, curtain closes.

SCENE THREE

Curtains open to reveal the train passengers sleeping. It is dark. Only a few lights twinkle outside the train.

MENTIGO
(offstage)
It's just up ahead, a few feet away.

CRYSTAL FAIRY, THISTLE, ROSITA THE BAT, and DIGGER DOG
(enter running and pointing excitedly at the train)
It's here! It's here! Digger Leader, it's here!

DIGGER LEADER SAM
(enters)
Look at the size of that thing.

*(The rest of the **UNDERGROUND CREATURES** enter and look around the train.)*

CUCKOO
Look at all the creatures in there.

THISTLE
Are they sleeping?

*(**DIVINE** begins to snore)*

CRYSTAL FAIRY
It sounds like it.

*(**CRYSTAL FAIRY** ,**THISTLE, ROSITA THE BAT**, and **DIGGER DOG** begin to laugh)*

DIGGER LEADER SAM
Quiet. Don't wake them up. They may be dangerous.

CREEPY CRAWLY
*(cautiously steps inside the train and crawls around. She walks up to **KEITH**)*
This must be their Wise One – the Elder.

THISTLE
*(walks up to **GERALD**)*
No this is the leader. He has more hair.

44

CUCKOO
*(walks towards **BOB** and picks up his dreads)*
He has hair too.

FRANK
*(walks to **MYRON**)*
But this one is wearing a uniform

MENTIGO
*(walks up to **CONDUCTOR CARL**)*
So is this one. Let's ask him

DIGGER LEADER SAM
Wait! We have to let the Supreme Judge know about this before
they wake up. A vessel from the top side does not magically
end up here. We have to find out why.

CREEPY CRAWLY
What if it was magic?

DIGGER LEADER
We still have to find out why they are here. What if these
"vessels" full of humans start showing up here. What are we
going to do?

ROSITA THE BAT
We can't be discovered.

DIGGER LEADER SAM
Alright. Crystal Fairy, Thistle, Rosita the Bat, and Digger Dog
you go to the Supreme Judge and report what we've found.
Digger Dog you're in charge.

DIGGER DOG
Yeah!!

DIGGER LEADER SAM

Crystal Fairy and Thistle, report back to me as soon as you've spoken to the Supreme Judge.

CRYSTAL FAIRY

We won't let you down.

THISTLE

Not this time.

DIGGER LEADER SAM

Cuckoo, Creepy Crawly, and Frank, you stay with me to keep an eye on the humans.

MENTIGO

What do I do? I want excitement, adventure…

DIGGER LEADER

Search for more vessels or signs of humans

MENTIGO

I'm on it

(CRYSTAL FAIRY, THISTLE, ROSITA THE BAT, DIGGER DOG, and MENTIGO exit)

DIGGER LEADER

You three stay close.

MENTIGO

We'll watch from the outside.

The four of them leave the train car and crouch outside. **GABBY** *and* **MYRON** *begin to wake up.*

GABBY
(begins to beat on her phone)
What's wrong with my phone? Hello? Hello?

MYRON

This does not compute. One moment I was having my delicious Italian Dunkers and the next minute I felt like I hadn't slept in years. What happened? *(looks outside window)* Where are we?

BOB

(yawns and stretches)

Wow! I have a headache.

KEITH

(sits up quickly, pats himself as if to make sure he's still there, then sighs)

Whew! Not dead yet.

LIZZIE

I feel like I've swam 100 miles. My arms and legs are so heavy *(stands up and begins to stretch)*.

Everyone begins to wake up one or two at a time.

DRACO

Where are we? I don't remember booking a gig this far south. Where's my phone? I have to check this out.

MARGE

(looking out window)

Where are we? It doesn't look like anyplace I've seen before.

DIVINE

Hey, the train is not moving.

DRACO

(runs to the window)

What do you mean the train is not moving?

LAUREN

The train is not moving? I'll never get to my lung specialist

47

CONDUCTOR CARL
No, no, nein, nunca, never!

GERALD
(begins to sing)
We're not moving any more
I say we're no moving no more
What did we stop for?
Wo Wo Wo
We're standing still
Ain't gonna move 'til
We get...

CONDUCTOR CARL
Stop singing songs sir. The train's in trouble.

DRACO
We're going to miss our next gig. We'll be sued for breaking our contract. It'll cost us millions *(pulls out cell phone)* I have to reach the promoter. Hello...hello!

GABBY
EMFBI, there's no signal. TMWFI.

BOB
What did you say?

DRACO
EMFBI Excuse me for butting in. TMWFI Take my word for it.

COO COO
You're saying there's no signal.

LAUREN
We're trapped! Soon we'll run out of oxygen then we'll –

LIZZIE

Calm down. We'll get out of here.

DIVINE

How? We don't know where we are or how we got here.

MORGANA

I'm scared.

KEITH
(Turns to MORGANA)

This is probably your fault. You probably rigged the train to stop here…wherever we are.

MORGANA

I have no idea what you're talking about.

COO COO
(turns to MORGANA)

What did you do? Why did you choose this train? What do you know?

LIZZIE

Why would she want to harm the train?

MARGE

Morgana follows The Volcanoes around everywhere they go. Everywhere.

MORGANA

Well I am The Volcanoes biggest fan and that's what big fans do. They follow their idols. *(turns to BOB. BOB moves away from MORGANA)* My favorite song is "Jam to the Center of the Earth".

GERALD

You all wrote that song? I like that one.

DIVINE

A big fan goes to every show. A CRAZY fan follows us after the concert, in our hotels, tries to get into our limo at the airport…

KEITH

It's as if she's one of the band.

CUCKOO
(outside of the train)
These humans are very boring.

DIGGER LEADER

We are here to observe only.

FRANK

Can't we go in there?

DIGGER LEADER

Absolutely not. We wait and watch out here.

LAUREN

If we don't get out of here we'll starve.

DRACO

Is there a fax machine on board? I have to get hold of the concert promoters.

LIZZIE

I need to get a hold of the swimming competition.

GABBY

BTW, can I PLS have something to eat? TYUM.

LAUREN
(gasps and grabs her head)
Oh no I think I'm having a stroke. I can't understand one word she's saying.

DRACO

You're fine. She's speaking in text message.

MORGANA

What does that mean?

MYRON

She spends so much time on the phone talking and sending text messages, she probably doesn't know any other way to speak to people without a cell phone.

DRACO

She asked if she could have something to eat.

DIVINE

Wait a minute. Food. I fell asleep right after I ate the Taco N Bag.

LAUREN

I only ate crackers because I had an upset stomach.

BOB

I had the Smiles.

CONDUCTOR CARL

Same supper. Malted Milk with Melted Marshmallows.

GERALD

First I ate pizza, then some marshmallows, then some more pizza, then some more mallows, and BAM! I was out like a light.

LIZZIE

All that dieting for nothing? *(Getting louder and louder)* I mean all the marshmallows I ate just went to my thighs with that long nap. Now we don't know where we are??? Does anyone care that I'm supposed to be swimming right now???

BOB
(laughing and drum rolling on the back of the seat in front of him)
Drum roll, please. Swimmer having issues. Swimmer having issues.

KEITH
(looking out window)
I haven't seen a sky this dark and foreboding since Antony and Cleopatra met.

BOB
How old ARE you?

LAUREN
Is there a pharmacy down here? I need to get my meds. I think I'm beginning to itch again.

COO COO
The most important thing is that my food did not cause this. Besides, these accusations are not getting us any closer to what happened.

MYRON
Maybe so but it seems like everyone suddenly fell asleep after eating. And now we're here.

CONDUCTOR CARL
Why? Where? Who?

KEITH
Calabar!!

LIZZIE
What is Calabar?

LAUREN
I hope that's a brand of painkillers because I'm getting a terrible headache.

KEITH

Calabar is an evil person.

BOB

I told you, you're seeing things. Calabar is not on this train.

KEITH

I know it was her. *(turns to the rest of the passengers)* Calabar was in our band in the early years.

DIVINE

She was nice enough but she couldn't play an instrument, sing, or write music.

DRACO

She did play the triangle

BOB

But she made great costumes. But when we stopped wearing matching costumes there was no place for her.

KEITH

So we asked her to leave but she thought we were kicking her out because we didn't like her. She hated us. She couldn't understand that we just wanted to do something different.

MORGANA

How exciting. This is like being in an episode of Behind the Music.

LIZZIE

But why would Calabar take the train?

CONDUCTOR CARL

(begins to cry)

Take the train. Horrible!! Hijack!

MARGE

She swore revenge. And she <u>always</u> did what she said.

GABBY
Hello, CMIIW –

DRACO
She said "Correct me if I'm wrong"

GABBY
The rest of us are not in the band. *(Pauses)* PU.

DRACO
PU means "This stinks"

GERALD
She's right. If Calabar wanted to get back at you, why did she take the whole train with all of us on it?

BOB
Maybe it was easier. Besides who says she was here?

LIZZIE
What does she look like?

DIVINE
She's about four feet tall with curly pinkish red hair.

GABBY
OMG!

DRACO
Oh my god!

GABBY
FWIW I saw her.

DRACO
For what it's worth… I saw her. Hold it! You saw her?

GABBY

I was talking to my friend Samantha and I saw his four foot girl was saying something about a solo world concert tour starting in Cairo at the base of the Sphinx. Oh, she also said she created the sound of The Volcanoes.

DIVINE

What are we going to do?

CRYSTAL FAIRY, THISTLE, ROSITA THE BAT, and DIGGER DOG return and crouch down next to DIGGER LEADER, CUCKOO, FRANK, and CREEPY CRAWLY.

DIGGER LEADER

What do you have to report?

CRYSTAL FAIRY

The Supreme Judge wants the humans taken to the council.

THISTLE

She wants to hear their story.

DIGGER LEADER

They certainly have an interesting one.

MENTIGO enters

CUCKOO

Did you find something?

MENTIGO

I think one of the humans escaped from the train and is tunneling back up to the surface.

DIGGER LEADER SAM

Maybe he discovered something and is about to tell the topside. We can't be discovered. We have to act now. Let's get together *(all the UGC huddle together).* CHARGE!!!!!! *(all the UGC's storm the train)*

FREEZE!!!!! *(everyone immediately stops)* In the name of the Supreme Judge of the Center of the Earth we order you to follow us to the Council.

LAUREN

Oh, I think I'm going to faint.

Blackout Curtains close

SCENE FOUR

*Curtains open to reveal a stage with all the **UNDERGROUND CREATURES** plus the Unicorn Centaur Judge **CENTA** in the middle. **CENTA** is in a long decorative robe. They are in a cave with several tunnels leading out of it. A **DRAGON BAT** sits at the side of **CENTA**. All the train passengers are standing in an area roped off on stage right. Everyone is speaking. Two mermaids enter from stage left of **CENTA**. They look like they are searching.*

LIZZIE

Where are we?

MYRON

From what I can gather, we are in the center of the Earth. That means we are probably more than a thousand miles below ground.

MARGE

But that means we had to pass through tons of rock and lava.

MYRON

The Charging Chunnel is the state of the art in train travel.

CONDUCTOR CARL

Terribly terrific train

MELINA

Morgana! Morgana! Where is my little guppy?

MORGANA

Oh no! It's my mother. I can't see her. Someone hide me.

MELINA

Oh no, no, no. Don't you try to hide from me missy. Morgana, what are you doing here?

MORGANA

Mom you're embarrassing me.

MELINA

Oh, I'm going to do a lot more than embarrass you. Tell me what's going on.

MAGGIE

Yeah Morgana *(sticks out her tongue at **MORGANA**)*.

MORGANA

Just stay out of this. It's between me and The Volcanoes

MELINA

I should have known. It just makes me so sad. *(begins to sing to the tune of Sunrise, Sunset))*
Is this the little guppy I spawned?

MELINA
(cont'd.)

Is this the little fish who swims?

CENTA

Everyone take your seats. I am Centa, the Supreme Judge of the Center of the Earth. I now call this Council meeting to order.

MAGGIE

Let's sit over there Mom.

MELINA

(begins to cry loudly)

Where did I go wrong?

CENTA

Friends of the council, we have a serious issue before us. Our esteemed Digger Leader and his crew discovered a strange vessel stuck in the northwest section of the Earth's core. Inside were several members of the topside earth race and one member of the topside aqua people. We can decide if they are invaders to our land and mean us harm or if they are simply friends who have lost their way. Digger Leader Sam.

DIGGER LEADER SAM

Yes maam?

CENTA

What is the condition of the vessel and the earth around it?

DIGGER LEADER SAM

The area surrounding the vessel is not beyond repair. As a matter of fact, there is now a new tunnel to the topside.

CENTA

That may be a good thing but that may cause problems as well. *(Walks to the train passengers)* You must understand. There are three worlds on this planet. The topside of the Earth, where you live. The underwater world and our world. The core of the Earth. Everyone who lives here does not fit into the other two worlds. We live here in harmony, deep beneath the surface and deep beneath the sea. We want to keep our ways of living. The topside world does not value its gifts or beauty that is there. Forgive us if we are suspicious, but we have learned that once you destroy part of your world, you seek to destroy others.

DIGGER LEADER SAM

The vessel is in good shape but it will take a while to remove it from where it lies. It is all metal and the magnetic field is too strong down here to allow us to dismantle the pieces.

CONDUCTOR CARL

Don't destroy the Charging Choo Choo!

CENTA

What about the passengers? The humans?

DIGGER LEADER

They all seem to be here.

MENTIGO

Sir, what about my report?

DIGGER LEADER

There may be one that has escaped.

MENTIGO

I saw signs of someone going through one of the other tunnels. They were headed topside.

All the **UNDERGROUND CREATURES** *gasp.*

KEITH

Calabar!

CENTA

Silence please.

KEITH

But you gotta understand. It was Calabar who did this. It was Calabar who is headed up to the top of the earth.

CENTA

What is this Calabar? And why do you have a mermaid with you?

MELINA

I told that girl she swims with the wrong crowd. Morgana, how many times did I tell you to stay in the reef? She hears that music and something gets into her.

MORGANA

Mom, I told you I'm old enough to go out on my own.

MELINA

And <u>this</u> is what happens. I am swimming at home, planting a new crop of seaweed. I'm just about to take your baby sister to the Giant Mussel Mall in Atlantis and I get a call on my shell phone. It is the Supreme Judge. Do you hear me Morgana? The <u>Supreme</u> Judge of the Center of the Earth. She wants to know why my mermaid daughter is stuck in a topside tin can with humans. If your father were alive he would shed a scale over this.

MORGANA

But it's The Volcanoes mom.

MELINA

I don't care if it's the Earthquakes or the Hurricanes or some other natural disaster. Do the Volcanoes put plankton on your table? Do the Volcanoes put coral over your head?

MAGGIE

Do you see what you're doing to this family? Mom is upset and crying and I'm supposed to be getting my tail shined for the big swim tomorrow night.

MORGANA

It's not my fault. She paid me.

CENTA

Who paid you?

MORGANA *hesitates.*

MELINA

Morgana Elizabeth Jones. What do you have to say?

MORGANA

It was Calabar.

The train passengers gasp.

MELINA and CENTA

Who is this Calabar?

DRACO

Miss Supreme Judge, Calabar used to be in our band but we had to let her go. She wasn't very happy. We think she wants to get rid of the band so she could take over our songs and now she plans a world tour.

CENTA

She seems more than "not very happy" to do something like this. There must be something more.

BOB

That's all. We just put her out of the band.

MORGANA

That is not all. I met Calabar when I was swimming in the Bermuda Triangle on a field trip. She saw my Volcanoes t-shirt and said she used to be in the band. Of course I didn't believe her. But she told me the whole story of how she used to play the triangle in the band and that she even made the costumes. She also played an old CD where she had a triangle solo. She even told me she wrote the song "Jam to the Center of the Earth".

CENTA

I love that song!

MORGANA
I felt sorry for her.

DIVINE
That's not true. She didn't write that song.

KEITH
Well, not really.

BOB
Well she did come up with the title.

DIVINE
But that's not the song.

BOB
Maybe…but we didn't give her credit for it.

LIZZIE
Well it doesn't matter now. We're stuck down here and we can't do anything about it.

LAUREN
It's not so bad. The temperature is clearing up my sinuses.

CRYSTAL FAIRY
Maybe on your next album you can write something special on the cover.

CUCKOO
Maybe dedicate the song to her.

CREEPY CRAWLY
You all can write a new song.

FRANK

You can call it "Tribute to a Lost Friend"

DRACO

That's a great idea. I'll call the record company right now and tell them about it.

GABBY

No reception remember?

DRACO

That's right. We want to make things right but we can't if we're stuck down here.

CENTA

Where is this Calabar now?

MORGANA

She's headed to Cairo for the big concert. I was supposed to follow her later but the band recognized me before I could sneak away.

CENTA

Digger Leader. Do we still have the express tunnel to Africa?

DIGGER LEADER

Yes. It was just serviced yesterday.

CENTA

I think we should help these people. It is clear that those that are at fault want to solve the problem and become better people. And the rest of you are innocent bystanders. But Morgana...

MORGANA

I am so sorry. I thought if I helped Calabar I would have a chance to get closer to my favorite band. I didn't mean to hurt anyone.

CENTA
I believe you. This should probably be handled now between you and your mother.

MELINA
We have a lot of talking when we get back to the reef young mermaid. But I'm glad you are safe.

CENTA
Dragon Bat.

DRAGON BAT
Yes sir.

CENTA
You are our best guide through our tunnels. Take these people straight to Cairo. Make sure you come out exactly under the Sphinx. For the rest of you, follow Dragon Bat closely. He moves quickly but there is no one better that can take you through the maze of tunnels we have created here.

LAUREN
A maze? I thought you said this was an express tunnel.

DRAGON BAT
But it's not fun if there is not a little adventure. Dragon Bat at your service. Follow me.

CENTA
Good luck everyone.

DRAGON BAT
Alright everyone. Follow me. Ready, set, GO!!!
Curtains close and the actors adlib traveling through the tunnels while the scene change occurs. Characters can say things like, "Wow, look at that lava." "Is it supposed to be so sticky down here?" "How much further?" "Just follow me",

etc. Curtains open after set has been changed. **CALABAR** *is standing in front of the Sphinx with several instruments around her.* **CALABARBIE** *appears to be tuning a guitar.*

DRAGON BAT
(offstage)
Almost there. Almost there. Here we go!!

Everyone but **CALABAR** *and* **CALABARBIE** *burst through the Sphinx*

KEITH
Hello Calabar.

CALABAR
What are you doing here? I sent you to the center of the Earth! How did you get here?

GABBY
WYLEI...

DRACO
She said, "When you least expect it"

GABBY
...we turn up *(cell phone rings)* Hello! Oh hi Samantha. OMG wait until you hear what happened to me *(walks stage left)*.

BOB
We're very sorry Calabar.

CALABAR
For what?
BOB
We should have given you credit for coming up with the title for "Jam to the Center of the Earth".

DIVINE

We're going to let the whole world know that you are a part of that song.

CALABAR

Are you serious? You're not trying to trick me?

COO COO

It's not a trick. It's true. They said it in front of everyone.

KEITH

We'll even announce it now in front of everyone at your concert.

DRACO

Brilliant marketing by the way.

LAUREN

What about the band getting back together and playing again?

MYRON

That's sounds great. The crowd would love it.

KEITH

We could need a little extra triangle.

GERALD

Do you think you need a little harmonica?

LIZZIE

I'm a great kazoo player.

COO COO

I'm coo coo for congas!

BOB

We always need more percussion.

DIVINE

What do you say Calabar?

CALABAR

This is happening so fast. I never wanted to hurt you ...but I was mad.

KEITH

You had a right to feel that way.

CALABAR

I probably should of handled things differently. Let me think about it. Alright. Let's do it.

DIVINE

Let's do jam to the "Center of the Earth" for old times sake.

ALL

YEAH!!!!!!!!!

Everyone picks up an instrument and begins to play the song. Curtains close.

Join
by Jonathon Bunton

There's something happening here
Not in one town,
Nor in a state,
And not in a country,
All over the world
Out of our
Ignorance
Things are dying
Their souls crying
And only out of us
Joining hands
Can we repel
What's coming.

Underwear For Sale
by Ben Woolford

Once there was a man who was walking around with a stack of underwear on his head, yelling, "Underwear for sale!" But no one came, so he cut through a backyard and came to a big oak tree. Then he took all the underwear off his head, and set them down right next to him. And he went to sleep…

When he woke up, he looked to the side of him but there was nothing there. Then he looked to the other side and there was nothing there either. Then he looked up into the tree and there were some elephants with underwear on their heads. The man said to them, "If you want that underwear you are going to pay me $5.50." They said, "No!"

While the man was sleeping it had rained. When the elephants reached up and felt the underwear on their heads, it was wet, so they threw them down! The man laughed so hard that he fell into the river never to be seen again.

Spring
by Rose Guardino

Spring
poppies
roses
internet
new
ground

Fried Chicken
by Vivian Livesay

Once upon a time there was a turkey. No, a duck! No, a seagull! No, an albatross! Wait! I have it!

Once upon a time there was a chicken. His name was Fried Chicken.

One day he was walking through the woods when something hot fell on his head. "The thun ith falling! The thun ith falling! (He had a lisp.*) I mutht tell the weatherman!" And he scurried off.

On his way to the weather house, he tripped over a sleeping snake and woke it up. "SSSSwhat have we hereSSSSS? Hey Fried ChickenSSSSSS have any newSSSSSSSSS?"

"The thun ith falling! I'm on my way to tell the weather man!

"I SSSSSSee, I SSSSSSSSwill come with youSSSSSS."

"Letth go."

On their way to the weather house they slipped in the mud and ran into a pig who was loungin' around in the mud. "Cccccccaaaaaw wha? What's that? (Yawn) come back later I'm trying to sleep Cccccccaaaaawwwwwwww."

"THE THUN ITH FAllING!!!"

"Wha? Okay, okay, now back it up and say it again in plain English!"

"I'm thpeaking plain English!"

"He meanSSSSSSSS," said the snake, "the SSSSSSSun iSSSSS falling."

"Wha? The sun is falling? I don't believe such foolishness."

"But it'th true! A peeth of it fell on my head!"

"You can do what you want, but I'm not coming. cccccccccaww."

So they walked on. When they got there, the weatherman was watching TV. "Come in," said the weatherman.

"What are you watching?" asked Fried Chicken.

"The news. What do you think I'm watching? Cartoon network?" Then they all watched the news. "Welcome back to the news with Jack Smith. Today, animals everywhere are dropping lit light bulbs out of trees.

"Oopth! I geth that's what fell on my head!"

THE

END

* A person who says S's as th

Sandwich
by Daniel Davila and Simon Schönemann-Poppeliers

A sandwich has layers just like a book
And when you see one lying around
You might just take a look.

For inside a sandwich
There might be something
Strange to behold
There might be a Zizzer snazzle's tail
With a piece of grey mold
Or a donkey's eyeball made of jelly.

Watch out it might be smelly
So make sure to plug your nose
That was the choice that we chose
So open up a sandwich and
See what you can see and

If you choose to leave it alone then let it be.

The Josh Charlie Story!
by Charlie Wagner and Josh Link

Once there were two boys who lived by a mansion that was haunted. Three weeks later they went inside the mansion but they got scared and ran out and ran home. They told their parents what happened. Their parents were surprised.

"Do you believe us?" the boys asked.

"No, we don't!" they replied.

"We'll show you proof," the boys screamed. They ran in the mansion, found a box, and ran home. They went to their room and opened the box.

Then something came out! Their parents came up the stairs. The ghost came out of the box and took over their parents. The two boys were fighting, because they thought they would die anyway. They heard footsteps, paused their rough housing, and saw their parents running down the stairs to take over the world!

They followed them down the stairs and the boys started counting …3, 2, 1. Then the boys darted out the window like a speeding bullet. They jumped, broke the window glass without getting a cut, jumped through and landed on their feet. That was a stupid idea for them to do! They then looked up, saw their parents, and started running after them.

They hid from them behind a bush, because they could have gotten killed. Cars were flying everywhere. Even people were flying, because their parents were already taking over the world!!! What were they going to do?

They dashed towards their parents. Then their parents hit them. They went flying into the bush. Now they were covered in blood, but they were not dead. They cried and cried and cried and then they saw a flash of light. It was a portal to another world! It sucked them in. They cried for help and then they noticed that they were in the past. They realized that they had to stop themselves from getting the box, so they ran in the mansion to stop themselves from getting the box. One knocked the other out, because he was acting weird.

71

He woke up and said, "What did you do that for?"

"I wanted to is why."

He said hi to some kids running up a hill and realized that it was them (they didn't realize it was really them.) They started chasing themselves to get the box but they got sucked into the portal. Then one of the boys threw a rock at them and he dropped the box. It rolled down the hill and he grabbed it and threw it in the mansion window. It landed right back were they found it and the portal closed.

They were in the present! They ran in the mansion and got the box and threw it out the window. It landed in the lake and a shark ate it. Now the ghost possessed the shark.

The End!! For now. Watch for the sequel.

Snow Black and the Seven Elves
by Sierra T. Reed

Once upon a time, there was a baby born, and her name was Snow Black. She was the daughter of Snow White and Prince Charming. Her skin was as white as could be, and she had hair as black as the blackest night. Her eyes were unbelievable, as blue as the bluest flower. Everybody loved her the instant they saw Snow Black. Her mother and father were very pleased and had a big feast in her honor.

She grew up to be very beautiful, and when she turned sixteen, men started courting her. Snow Black; however, did not like any of them, but the instant they saw her, the men fell in love. Her mother and father wanted her to pick one, marry, and have children. 'Well', she thought, 'I don't want any of them.' So Snow Black ran off into the woods, and she sat down on a curious little stump and began to cry.

"I don't want to get married!" she moaned. The little stump moved. Then Snow Black said, "Who are you?" For Snow Black knew that it would be rude to say 'what are you' instead of 'who are you.'

The little stump said, "I am the respectable door to the house of a very honorable elf named Nimblefoot, and my name is Oakendoor." Oakendoor asked, "What's your name?"

"Hickoryleaf," answered Snow Black, picking her favorite tree. "Can I come in?"

"For a very gorgeous lady as yourself, I'll let you come in."

"Thank you, Oakendoor," said Snow Black. " Oakendoor opened. Snow Black stepped inside the doorway, and gasped at what she saw. There were seven elves seated at the table, all of them as fair as can be. There were three female elves and four male elves. One, she noticed was very handsome and more richly dressed than the others. He was the one who spoke to her.

"I see Oakendoor let you in, and he very rarely does. Sit down and eat with us," he said.

"Is your name Nimblefoot?" Snow Black asked.

"Yes."

Snow Black also noticed that the elven ladies were as beautiful as or more beautiful than she was. "No wonder people call elves the Fair Folk," she thought. "What a sight for mortal eyes."

Nimblefoot took her hand and took her to the table. They fell in love and got married a year later. They eventually had children, and Snow Black made friends with the elven ladies and here are their names: Brambletoe, Berryfeet, and Timberwolf. And she never told Nimblefoot her real name, but she did tell her friends.

The End

Mornings
by Kaiya Eleanor Grundmann

Mornings,
You wake up,
Birds singing their song,
Sun rays blaring through your window,
The alarm clock ringing,
Waiting for you to press the off button,
Lying in bed waiting
For your strength to help you get up.
You walk down the stairs
To the strong smell of breakfast.
Feeling the wind flowing onto your legs
From the shorts you wore to bed last night.
You sit down in your chair to eat;
Waiting until you can get into that warm morning shower,
Already feeling the water
Hitting your back,
Your mother putting the pancakes in front of you;
Eating slowly
So you don't miss the spongy good taste of your pancakes.
Walking into the bathroom and putting your towel
On the back of the toilet,
So you don't have to walk into the hall.
Freezing cold, you get into the shower and turn the heat
All the way up, getting yourself as wet as you can
Until the heat of the water runs out.
You get out of the shower cold,
Put on your towel and walk into your bedroom,
Opening your closet to the jungle of clothes,
Trying to find the perfect thing to wear;
Sliding your pants up your wet leg, then your shirt;
Your pants already wet from the wetness of your hair
Streaming down your bare back;
Going into the living room and slip on your backpack;
Kissing your mom goodbye as your dad has already

Gone to work,
You hear the bus coming near,
You run out the door like you're running the marathon,
About to cross the finish line,
You run up the path and into the bus.
That is when
Your morning ends.

The Food Decision
by Lucia Davila and Olivia Hurley

One day Eleanor was doing her homework, when her mom said, "It's time for lunch." Eleanor came to the table.

"What are these little green things?" she asked.

"Peas," said her mom.

"I think I am not hungry," said Eleanor. "I think I will go to Emily's house for lunch instead. She will have something good to eat," said Eleanor.

But at Emily's house they had pizza. In the pizza there were brown things. "What are these little brown things?" Eleanor asked Emily.

"Mushrooms," said Emily.

"I don't like mushrooms," they said together.

Eleanor and Emily said, "Let's go to Jill's house to eat.

"Bye mom," said Emily. Emily and Eleanor went to Jill's house. At Jill's house they were having chili.

Eleanor said, "If we don't like anything at each other's house, we should go to a restaurant."

They ended up going to the China Buffet and had everything.

The End

My Mama & Me
by Akilah Cannon and Emily Ireland Toal

Chapter One
April 22, 1930
Introducing You

Hi! My name is Jolene Donavan, and I am eight and one half years old. My Mama's name is Stacey Joe…well…that's what my Grandma Francine calls her when she is Mad at her or somethin'. Oh right, how rude of me. I forgot to introduce you to Frannie. She is my favoritest doll in the world! I had her for 6 years, and she is real special! My Papaw's name is Joe. My Pa's name is Jean.

There is a problem with Papaw. Mama says it is nothing for a young girl like me to be hearin' and that's not fair, 'cause he is my Papaw. But I guess I will find out when I am old enough. Anyway my Pa and Mama got in a real big fight last night, and it scared me real bad. I just kind of thought they loved each other, but just like Mama said "I need to keep my little nose out of their business" and dats what I intend on doin'. I'm just gonna stay out of it like a good girl …but I just gotta know…its killin' me!

Chapter Two
April 24, 1930
The Bigger Fight

Well, today is Jamie Marie's birthday Party. I made her the bestest present in the world. I made her a red friendship bracelet. I wish I had Made it for me, but as long as it Makes me happy…I mean…her happy….

Well, today is Jamie Marie's birthday party. I made her the bestest present in the world. I made her a red friendship bracelet. I wish I had made it for me, but as long as it makes me happy. I mean.her happy. The worst thing happened today after the party. Grandma Francine told me that Pa hit Ma real, real hard across the face, and Ma fell and hit her head on the end of the

76

table. It started bleeding. Then Grandma Francine called the police, and Pa went

away while Ma went to the hospital.After Grandma Francine told me what happened I slowly walked up to my room and grabbed Frannie and holded her tight. I told her about everything good and bad that happened. Then I slowly fell asleep with Frannie on my lap still comfortin' me.

Chapter Three
April 25, 1930
The Next Day

I woke up with Frannie still in my lap. I walked downstairs, and I didn't see Mama. I ran into GrandMa Francine's house, and she wasn't there. I called the hospital, and they told me that GrandMa and Mama was there. They sent over a taxi that came and picked me up, so when I got to the hospital the fat lady at the desk was kind of scary but she was nice. I asked for Ms. Stacey Joe. She gave me a note that said room 315, and off I went like a race horse! As soon as I got to the room I knocked very politely and I said "Mama, Mama."

I heard a faint voice say, "Come in Jolene." So I walked into the room and I saw Grandma Francine & Mama.

GrandMa Francine said, "I am sorry I left you at the house. It was just that you were asleep, and I didn't want to disturb you."

"Well, that was fine, but couldn't you have left me a note or something?" I said.

"Well, yes, I am sorry."

Chapter Four
April 28, 1930
Moving

Well, the worst thing is happening today. Me and Mama are moving, and it is really sad. The worst thing is we are moving into the biggest place in the world -New York City! And the truth is I am really scared that I will never see my Pa again. I mean I know that he hurt Ma and all, but I will always love my Pa even if I don't like what he does. Same goes for my Mama. Oh gosh darn it! I just forgot about Jamie Marie. I was supposed to meet her at the Park this afternoon at 1:30, and I turned to look at the time and it is 2:12.

GrandMa Francine said, "Run child ya don't wanna be any later than ya already are!"

"Ok, love you," I said.

"You, too, darling. Bye now."

I ran out the door faster than fast itself. When I got down to the Park I said, "Hello, Ms. Jamie Marie. I am so sorry I am late. It's just my Ma and Pa and I don't know what to do."

"Well," said Jamie Marie, "I don't know what to do either unless you tell me what happened. Now you just kick that funny lookin' frown off your face and give me a smile."

"Oh, Jamie Marie, I wish it was that easy to tell," I said.

"Well, I got a while before Ma wants me in for supper," Jamie Marie said. "Alright, I guess I will have to tell you," I said with a sigh.

As I went on and on about what happened I saw Pa walkin' up the hill. I ran away as fast as I could, sayin' 'bye at the same time. Now that is hard! He finally caught up to me, and he said, "Let's go have a little chat."

Chapter Five
April 29, 1930
A Little Chat

"So how is your mother?" Pa asked.

"She is fine, but she officially hates you! And I don't like you either. You hurt my Ma, and you expect us to like you. Oh, I don't think so!!"

"Oh, watch your mouth!" said Pa. "Now, I know no one in your house likes me, but I am still your Pa, and you shall respect me."

"Why? You're just a big 'Ol bag of *doodoo* on a front porch getting burned."

"Man, you're even worse than Sally the Sow on a hot day in

heat!" I screamed.

"Then if you hate me so much, tell me you don't love me."

"Well, Pa that's the thing. I do love you. It's just I don't like the things you do at all, so you might as well go about your way again ok? And I think it is best that you never come around here again. It's for the best, ok?"

"Well, honey I can't do that. Ya see a long time ago your mother did some things that she regrets. And well, you are legally mine so I can't leave you here. So you can't go to New York with your Mama."

"Pa I am going to go get Ma and I'm gonna tell on you!"

"That is fine, and while you are there get your bags. I will be with your Ma in the living room."

"Fine, but I'm gonna put up a fight!"

"Oh you better not, little missy!"

"Ok sir!" Jolene said sarcastically.

Pa walked over the hill to the house. I was trailing along behind him mumbling I hate this, I hate this.

When we got home I saw Mama crying but not sobbing. Pa said "Go get your things, honey."

"But Pa, I don't wanna. I am not going to leave Mama. It's not fair that you are Making me do this. I am not leaving Mama never ever!" I said with water in my eyes.

"It's ok darling, I'll get you back I promise." Mama said hugging me.

"Ok, Mama," Jolene said skeptically.

Chapter Six
April 31, 1930
Court Day

Well, today me, Mama, and Pa are going to this place called court. I am really scared 'cause I don't know what that place is, but Mama says there is nothin' to be scared of. So we get there, and there is this freaky lookin' guy with a dress- thing on and white hair! He looks like a girl with that dress on, but that's just me. Anyways, after court Pa was lookin' like he was about to cry, and I'm not sure why.

I asked him and he said, "Well, you are going to live with your Mama in New York City, and so, I'm not going to see you again. I will always love you."

"Yes! I will always like you, too," Jolene replied bouncily. I ran over to Mama and gave her a big ol' hug. "You did it Mama!" I said very happy.

"No, <u>we</u> did it," Mama said, still huggin' and comfortin' me.

Chapter Seven
May 5, 1930
Moving

Mama and me finally got all of our stuff packed. We are moving to the big city. I am so scared 'cause we are moving into this one neighborhood where all the rich peoples live, and I hate snobby rich peoples. Mama says I will make friends fast, but I think otherwise, because I am not like anyone else here. Oh yeah, and the snobby rich kids have New York accents, and I think they sound funny. I just hope I don't get their accent!

At school we have to wear uniforms and my uniform is a plaid skirt, a white button up shirt with a jacket over it that has a icon thing of a lion and a snake in the right corner. It is really freaky. Mama says I look really cute with it on, but she always says that even when she hates it. She says that when I'm not around. It's really hard not see Pa anymore, but I guess I will have to get through it; the good news is that I made a new friend. His name is James Ellington, III, and he is not as snobby as everyone else. The bad news is…

Chapter Eight
May 7, 1930
Mama's New "Friend"

Mama has a new "friend." His name is Carter S. Flamingo, and he works in advertising at Mama's new work called the New York Post Newspaper! She really likes him, and I think he might replace Pa. He is really nice, and he bought the prettiest doll house for Frannie. Sometimes I wish he was my Pa in the first place.

I think that Mama really likes him, but like Mama has said before, I have to mind my own business. They have been spending a lot of time together, and they have been going to a lot of fancy restaurants. Mama ain't use t' going places like that 'cause Pa never took her anywhere fancy. I really think Carter and Mama like each other more than friends, 'cause they spend a lot of time together, and he comes over a lot, too.

When James came over "Pa really"...oh sweet nibblets... I just called him "Pa!" I think it might be ok to call him Pa...I'm not sure. Anyways, when James came over I showed him my room, and I showed him the beloved Frannie. He thought that she was real neat, and he liked the doll house Carter bought, too.

I didn't want James to leave, but his Mama said that he had to go take his weekly piano lessons. James said he rather be here with me and Frannie, but he had to listen to his Mama and go. I heard that those lessons cost a fortune! Sometimes when I get real sad, I think about Pa and what he is doin' right that second, and I wonder if I'm ever gonna see him again. I'm really not sure if I wanna see him again after what he did to Mama. No one would want to talk to him or see him again if this happened to them, but I just want to have another chat with him again.

Chapter Nine
May 9, 1930
School Time

Well, school is doing fine. Well, actually it is not so great, 'cause there are these girls who act like those ones you hear on the radio. Me and James call them the mean girls! They make fun of us all the time, and they say things like "you don't match" and "you and your little boyfriend needs to get out of our way," and after they say mean things like that, they put their fingers together and go "Owwww tssssss!" The leader of the mean girls is Catalina. She is the worst of them all! I wish I could just zap them away to their own little *lala land* where everyone is just so perfect and everyone has a new outfit everyday and has...ok, so I am working myself up too much about this, but they just make me so mad!

Me and James always make impressions of them, and put our fingers together, and do that annoying thing, and we do it right in their faces! Now take that - you big crazy mean girls!

Well anyways, today is the school's talent show! Me and Jamie Marie use t'sing together in the talent show at my old school, but now that she moved I guess that I will have to do it all by myself. I guess for the talent show I will sing Amazing Grace! It is my favoritist song in the world! After I'm done singing everyone will clap and whistle like they were a big group of wild animals trying to catch their prey.

James is actually very good at playing the piano. I would never be able to play somthin' like that 'cause of the music that they play. There are all these notes and things that I just ain't good at readin'. Mama says readin' notes is what famous singers do, but I don't want to even try 'cause it looks too confusin'! Although when me and Frannie sit on my bed and listen to the radio and I hear really good jazz singers that Mama says I could be like, but when I grow up I think about it. They must have an awful hard life cause they always get the Papa...Papara... Paparazzi. I think that what they called.

I ain't got no clue what I wanna do when I am older like Mama is. I guess I will have to wait until then.

Chapter Ten
May 15, 1930
GrandPa Joe

Mama has been on the phone talking to grandma a lot and asking questions like, "Is he ok?" and "what is he doing now?" I wonder why Mama is so worried? It kinda' scares me. Anyways, Mama wants to go see Papaw, but she doesn't want me to go 'cause if we encounter Pa... Ya' see in school I am learning new words like *encounter* and *supercalifragilisticexpialidocious*. I am starting to lose my accent, but Mama isn't, trust me Mama isn't. Sometimes I worry about Frannie and Mama and Papaw because, well, it gets hard 'cause Frannie misses our old house and Jamie Marie, and the smell of our farm with pigs, horses & ducks. And Mama misses it too but most of all she misses Papaw for some odd reason. I have been trying to get the truth out of Mama about Papaw but nothing ever works with her.

Hold on she is knocking on my door. Oh my goodness I can't believe she told me... Oh my, I think I'm gonna cry until I can't cry no more. Oh no, this can't be happening - not to me, not to Papaw, not to no one. Papaw is dyin' of cancer! Me and Frannie can't believe this! So this is what they have been hiding from me all this time, and now it's getting worse! Maybe I shouldn't know...I think it's ok I didn't know. I'm not sure what I think right now 'cause everything is falling apart. Oh, I feel so bad that we left Papaw there all by himself with GrandMa. Sometimes I wish we would be back into the old house where I could be myself, and I wish Pa wouldn't have done what he did, so we could be one big happy family again. But I guess it doesn't work out that way. Even though I wish it would.

Chapter Eleven
May 21, 1930
No Papaw

We are going to see Papaw today in the hospital. Mama said I could even skip school. I told James the day before that I wouldn't be there today. FINALLY we are here... that was a real long ride! Oh no! The fat lady from the front desk still works here. "Hi," I said, "We are here to see my Papaw Joe. May we have his room number?"

"Well, yes, you may. Here you go. The room number is 320 - right down the hall."

"Thank you," I said, "Hey Mama, that is five rooms in front of the one you were in. You remember?"

"Yes I remember darlin' and I wish I didn't," Mama said very sadly. We walked in to room 320 and it smelt' like fresh oranges that just came from the orange tree.

As soon as I saw Papaw I began to cry. "Please don't go, Papaw, please don't! I need you, Papaw!" I said with tears running down my face like a waterfall. I grabbed his hand and promised that I wouldn't let go.

"Daddy, I love you, and you will always be right here," Mama said pointing to her heart and with tears in her eyes.

"Papaw I am never letting you go! Never ever! Not even the good Lord can make me!"

The fat lady comes into the room and says very softly "Mr. Donavan. It is time for your surgery."

The fat lady waddled over to the bed and started to roll the bed out of room when I finally said, "No Papaw! Don't go! NO!"

Mama pulled me away while I was crying like I had never cried before. "It's ok, Jolene. Just have faith that he comes back. It's alright, it's alright. I will miss him too."

Chapter Twelve
May 21, 1930
Did He Make It?

We waited and waited for Papaw to get out of surgery. Finally one of the doctors came out of the surgery room and told us the news. "Did he make it, did he?" I said waiting for a good answer.

"Well," said the doctor, "The cancer spread."

"Well, how did it do that?" asked Mama.

"It went to his lymph nodes, and it spread through his whole body. We couldn't do anything about that. I am very sorry for your loss Ma'am," said the doctor and he walked away.

Mama started crying, and it was like she couldn't stop, not at all and me and Frannie just sat there thinking. We sat there for three hours until Mama said it was time to go home. On the way out of the hospital one of the doctors stopped us and started talking to Mama about Papaw and how he felt real bad 'cause he couldn't do anything more and that sort of stuff. Mama said "Thank you very much for trying," and walked away with not one expression on her face.

2 years later...

Well, it has been two years since Papaw died and I am now ten! GrandMa lives with us. And Carter and Mama got married. Now I gots myself a new little sister named Allison Marie, and she has to be the cutest baby in the entire world. James and I are thinking about getting married, but Mama says I got to be older before that can happen. So we are all finally happy, and we realized that it was ok for Papaw to go. It was the right time, and as you can tell I have almost lost my accent, but I don't plan on getting a new one anytime soon. I haven't seen Pa yet, but I think he is doing ok. We don't think about him a whole lot 'cause all Mama remembers is what he did. Anyway we go and see Papaw's grave everyday. We had him buried in the backyard under the oak tree. I am really happy now, but sometimes I wish it was just Mama & me!

Winter
by Rose Guardino

In winter
The snow is untouched until
A caravan of laughing children
Parades up the hill to sled
And play

In winter
There are igloos and
New white snow for
Today.

Evergreen trees and
Red-hot fires in
The evenings.

Fire
by Emily Hurley

Flickering
Flaming
Licking
Kissing
Reaching
Destroying everything in its path
Until it reaches the water
It spreads parallel to the water
And then...
The silent stillness envelops everything
The fire burned itself out
Everyone staring at the destruction

Cowboy Mouse
(El Ratoncito Vaquero)
By Nancy Armstrong, Erika Avila, Leo Avila, Diana
Cortes, Jorge Cortes, Ulises Cortes, Carmen Garcia, Xuli
Liu, Efigenia Magno, Alba Moreno, Joel Moreno, Cristina
Perez, Blanca Reyes, Rosa Rodriguez, Adriana Rosales,
Elva de Santiago, Maria de Santiago, Osiel de Santiago,
Edgar de Santiago, Viridiana de Santiago, Jing Angelina
Zhang

ACT I

(Mouse is on stage. Mother Mouse is waiting for him just off stage).

Mouse: Ahhh...it smells delicious. Chocolate and cheese! I think I am going to find out where that wonderful smell is coming from
(Mouse goes to kitchen)

Mouse: Surprise! What do my eyes see? A chocolate cake, and CHEESE!
(Mouse bites cake and cheese)

Mouse: That was delicious. Now I'm tired- a little nap would be nice.
(Mouse goes to sleep. Then wakes up.)

Mouse: Oh my goodness- it's so late! My mother will be waiting for me!

(Mother Mouse enters calling:)

Mother Mouse: Little Mouse! Where are you? It's late! I'm worried about you!

Mouse: Here I am. I'm sorry!

Mother Mouse: What have I told you? NEVER be late home!

Mouse: Well, I was at that girl's house again.

Mother Mouse: Again?

Mouse: I went there again because I smelled the cake- so rich and moist- and cheese too!

Mother Mouse: Did you eat any of it?

Mouse: Well maybe, just a little, but I was so hungry! I couldn't help it.

Mother Mouse: If this happens once more you will be in serious trouble.
(Mouse and Mother Mouse hide on-stage).

Girl: Mom, Mom! I'm home! Can I have something to eat?

Girl's Mom: Sure, there's chocolate cake and cheese in the kitchen.

Girl: Yum! ..... Mom, I can't find anything!

Girl's Mom: I can't believe it- there must be a huge mouse around here!

Girl: I'm going to catch him! Here kitty, kitty, kitty!

Cat: Meow!

Girl: I need you to help me catch a chocolate-stealing cheese-eating mouse!

Cat: I will help you eat him!

Girl: Cat, you never help do anything. I'll catch him myself if I have to stay up all night!

(Cat leaves. Girl sets up trap, hides, and waits for Mouse. Mouse comes in sniffing for food, falls into trap.)

Girl: Aha! I caught you!

Mouse: Let me go!

Girl: What are you saying? I can't understand anything you say!

Mouse: Please oh please oh please let me go! I didn't mean to do anything wrong. It's just that chocolate cake and the cheese smelled sooooooo good- I couldn't resist!

Girl: What? You must be speaking English. I can't understand you a bit. You stay right here in the trap. I'm going to feed you to my cat.

Mouse: No, no, no, no! Oh no! I don't want to die so young. I'm still a little mouse! My mother will be so upset if you do that!

Mouse Mother: Tell her to let you out!

Mouse: I told her to let me out but she can't understand me!

Girl: Mom! I caught the mouse but he's talking and I can't understand a word he says!

Girl's Mom: What does it sound like?

Girl: It sounds like English.

Girl's Mom: I think you had better go to the library and find some books to help you understand him.

(Girl exits. Cat enters.)

ACT II:

Cat: That **is** a juicy mouse! I'm so excited- I want to eat him!

(Grandmother comes in with a pot.)

Grandmother: I have a pot to make YOU into soup!

Mouse: Before you eat me, there's something you need.

Cat and Grandmother: What do we need?

Mouse: You need onions, salsa, and tomatoes!

Cat: But I don't like salsa.

Grandmother: I do! I'll eat you! I'll go buy all of those things so I can make you into soup.

Cat: Now that she's gone, I'll eat you!

(Mother Mouse comes up behind Cat.)

Mouse: Look, there is a bigger mouse behind you.

Mother Mouse: Yes! Come eat me instead.

(Cat runs to eat Mother Mouse, Cat falls into trap.)

Cat: Hey! You caught ME!

Mother Mouse: Don't try to escape. You have to pay for all the times you have frightened me and my children.

(Mother Mouse turns on the stove.)

(Cat escapes from the trap but falls into the pot).

Mouse: Alright! Cat soup!

Cat: I'm getting out of here!
(Mother Mouse puts lid on pot saying:)

Mother Mouse: No you don't!
(Grandmother returns from market carrying onions, salsa and tomatoes. Mother Mouse hides)

Grandmother: Mmmmmm! This soup is already looking delicious. And I see fur and whiskers in it- that mouse must have jumped in the pot himself. I'll just add these other ingredients. First the onions...

Cat: I hate onions!

Grandmother: Then the salsa.

Cat: Hot salsa- I can't stand it!

Grandmother: And the tomatoes.

Cat: I'm allergic to tomatoes!

Grandmother: Now I'll turn up the heat.

Cat: Noooooooo! Let me out of this pot!
(Cat throws off lid and jumps out of pot).

Grandmother: You're a cat! My soup pot must be magic- it turned a mouse into a cat! Here kitty, kitty... let me dry you off with my apron.
(Grandmother dries Cat off and sets it on her lap.)

Grandmother: Now let's you and I have a nice pot of vegetable soup together.

Cat: I'd rather have mouse soup.

Grandmother: What? Forgotten that you were a mouse already? I'll give you a nice bowl of chocolate milk instead.

Cat: Meeeeeeeow! That sounds good!
(Cat, Grandmother, Mouse and Mother Mouse).

ACT III

Scene I:

(Girl, Cow, and Dog are on stage.)

Girl: Let's go to the library. Would you like to go with me?

Cow: Mooo. I would like to go find some recipes for making ice cream and cheese.

Dog: Yes, I would like to go to the library to find some books about exercise.
(They go to the library. Librarian and English teacher are waiting. Dog jumps on the table and smells all the books.)

Librarian: What are you doing in the library, Dog?

Dog: I'm looking for exercise books.

Cow: Excuse me, could you help me to find a book about making ice cream and cheese?

Librarian: Right this way. Don't smell the books, Dog. Read them!

Girl: I want to learn English. Do you have a book that can help me?

Librarian: I can find two English tutors for you. They will show you lots of books.

Librarian: Miss Jenny! Oh Miss Jenny! Mr. Ulises, Oh

Mr. Ulises! Please come here.

Girl: Nice to meet you, Miss Jenny and Mr. Ulises.

Mr. Ulises: Glad to meet you too. How can I help you?

Miss Jenny: Glad to meet you. How can I help you?

Girl: I caught a mouse and he's speaking English. I can't understand him. Will you help me learn English please?

Mr. Ulises: Absolutely.

Miss Jenny: Absolutely.

Mr. Ulises: Let's go to your house and listen to what the mouse is saying.

Miss Jenny: Let's go to your house and listen to what the mouse is saying.

Girl: Great! Before we go I will call my dog and my cow. Cow! Dog! Come check out your books and let's go home!

Cow: Look! I found a recipe for strawberry mango ice cream!

Dog: Look at the book I found- I'm going to be a body builder dog. I bet I can lift up the Cow- watch me!

Cow: Noooooooo- DON'T DO THAT! Maybe after you eat some of my strawberry mango ice cream you'll be strong enough.
(They all go home.)

Scene II:

Mouse: Let me out! You can't keep me in jail. I want to see my lawyer!

Mr. Ulises: Calm down. Let's talk about it.

Miss Jenny: Calm down. Let's talk about it.

Girl: That mouse stole my cheese and chocolate cake.

Mouse: I'm sorry. I just ate a little bit. Here, I will give you my banana.

Girl: What did the mouse say?

Mr. Ulises: He said he will give you his banana.

Miss Jenny: He said he will give you his banana.

Girl: That's my favorite! It's a deal. Hey, Dog, are you strong enough to lift up the trap?

Dog: Yeah Watch me! I'm super dog!
　　　(Dog lifts up trap. Mouse comes out.)

Mother Mouse: Oh thank you! I promise you, he will never steal again.

Girl: I hope he will visit me so I can practice my English.

Mouse: Okay, sure.
Girl: In fact, if you help me learn English, I'll give you chocolate cake.

Mouse: And cheese?

Girl: Yes, and cheese too.

Cow: Who would like some raspberry-banana ice cream?

EVERYONE: WE WOULD! We scream, you scream, we ALL SCREAM FOR ICE CREAM!
　　(Music, party, dance.)

THE END

In the Spring Time
by Zack Vonderschmidt

In the spring time
Violets bloom
Bluebirds and cardinals chirp
Kids play outside –
Football - baseball
People swim.

In the spring time
The weather is in 70s, 80s
The snow melts.
The grass is green.

In the spring time
My grandparents come home
From Florida.
It won't be long
'Til I swim in Lake Monroe;
Kids go to the zoo.

Dive
by Olivia Dagley

Dive into the
 Ocean
         Of life
                White

White
                Light

Light
                So right

So right

blank
                dark

ocean of
        death
Wrong
                Wrong

So wrong
                Dark
                Dark
        Circle of life

                You're like
                A tree
In a forest
 Until the lightning
        Shoots you down
  Fall
                Fall

    Falling on the ground
        Forever

What I'm Going to Do for Spring Break
by Benny Luo

I'm going to go see the acrobats
And I'm going to Indianapolis tomorrow, Saturday,
With my mother.
I'm going to go to the children's museum, too.
I'm going to ride a carousel. I want to ride a white horse,
Then I'm going home to eat dinner.
We'll probably have asparagus spears and golden French fries
With barbequed pork for an entrée.
And then I'll go to sleep in the nighttime.
And that's all.
That's a lot for one day of spring break.

The Smart Dragon
by Walter Guardino

Once there was a reeeeeeeeeeally smaaaaaaaaaaart dragon named Smartdrag. Unfortunately he got stuck between a princess and a prince who hated each other. One day Smartdrag got tired of having to avoid flying bombs. So he came up with a plot to get rid of them.

One day while they were throwing bombs, he snuck into the princess' and the prince's land and breathed fire on it. He was a very smart dragon and it worked. The princess and the prince got so mad at each other that they jumped off a cliff.

The end

Silence
by Jonathan Bunton and Spencer Diersing

Silence
A quiet minute with no noise
No sound, No movement
But it is hard to find
Yet you really look
And you see it and exclaim
In happiness
I see it! I found silence!
But then you realize you were fooled, tricked
For your exclamation shattered
The silent minute
And you weep
Because it is finally silent
And then you smile to yourself
Proud that you finally
Are worthy of silence
So you lay back and watch
As the day takes its course
The sun sets
And then you know
This is perfect
And silence comes again
Weaving in and out of the day
Like a snake
Slithering around you
And it surprises
You know that
But you don't mind
You just smile as the silence engulfs you
Silence is a gift
The gift of being able to relax
And sleep a silent sleep
If only for a minute
That minute is glorious

A rebel of noise
An enemy of discomfort
You slip into a deep Slumber
If only for a minute
But if you look
You can find an ongoing silence
That petrifies the heart
And shakes your bones
You resent that
And try to yell
But you are muted
Trapped in the never ending silence
Without a sound
And after years
You have finally understood
The true sound
Of a whisper

Going To Florida
by Gabriel Bruner

March 10th:

When we were going to our aunt's house we saw two deer, one armadillo, and one fox. We slept there and the next day we saw two giant horses. We fed them four carrots and they ate them in one minute. We also saw a rabbit and we saw armadillos. Me and Michael got deer skulls.

March 11th

We got to feed the chickens and we held a really cute one. We saw a butterfly with a broken wing. We took care of it.

March 12th

We saw a train and it had 123 cars on it. On March 11th we got to ride on a four- wheeler.

March 13th

We went to an ocean and there were giant waves. We saw sharks. It was the Gulf of Mexico. We got buried in the sand. The sand was white, and we found lots of shells. In the morning I found a swamp and Michael, my brother, was holding out chips and waiting for the seagulls to come. He was trying to catch them.

March 14th

We went to the ocean again. First, we went to Black Water River, and we had little pancakes for breakfast. We had eggs and apples. On the way to the river we saw two turtles.

We went on a hike in the woods, and we saw an alligator. It was raining. Then it rained harder and we stayed in the tent all day and watched movies and ate food.

March 15th

We went hiking again, and we went to the sand. We went in

the water and went tubing in the water. One mile in the water. We went all the way to Black Water River, and we went to the ocean again. We went next to the water and my dad made a wall of sand.

March 16th
    We are leaving today. The end.

Printed in the United States
76893LV00002B/1-150